24045

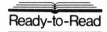

The Lucky Man

By Mary Blount Christian

Illustrated by Glen Rounds

MACMILLAN PUBLISHING CO., INC.
New York
COLLIER MACMILLAN PUBLISHERS
London

Macmillan Publishing Co., Inc.
866 Third Avenue, New York, N.Y. 10022
Collier Macmillan Canada, Ltd.
Printed in the United States of America

10   9   8   7   6   5   4   3   2   1

Library of Congress Cataloging in Publication Data
Christian, Mary Blount.   The lucky man.
   (Ready-to-read)
   Summary: The cumulative catastrophes of hard-luck Felix land
him in court where a wise judge's decisions prove him a lucky man.
   [1. Justice — Fiction]   I. Rounds, Glen, *date*.   II. Title.
PZ7.C4528Lu   [E]   79-11024   ISBN 0-02-718270-3

To the Rosenfelds: Arnold, Ruth, Bill,
Jon and Lauren

Chapter One

Rich Brother, Poor Brother

Once there were
two brothers.
Their farms were
side by side.

Marcos was rich.
But Felix was poor,
and the harder
he worked,
the poorer he got.

Felix lived in a house
that creaked in the wind
and leaked in the rain.
Marcos had given it to him.

But as Marcos got richer,
he got more selfish.
One day he said,
"I want my house back.
I will keep my pigs in it."

Felix showed Marcos
a piece of paper.
"It says the house
is mine," he said.
"You signed it, too."

"The paper means nothing,"
Marcos yelled.
"No one else knows
about it.
I will go to the city.
The judge there will make
you give the house to me."

Felix was scared.
Maybe Marcos was right.
Then his family would have
no place to live.

He decided to see
the judge, too,
and show him
the piece of paper.

11

Chapter Two

Onions For Two

Felix kissed
his family good-by.
His wife gave him
a cooking pot and
four onions.
It was all they had.

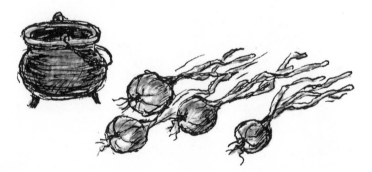

It took two days
to walk to the city.
The first day
Felix walked until dark.
He came to a farmhouse.

"May I have
a little water?"
he asked the farmer.
"And a place to sleep?"

"You may have
one cup of water.
And you may sleep
with my dogs,"
the farmer said.

Felix stepped inside
the farmhouse.
The table was covered
with food.
The farmer's wife
sat eating.

While the farmer and
his wife ate,
Felix cooked his onions.
"Umm," the farmer's wife said.
"They smell good.
I want one."

Felix put an onion
on her plate.
"May I have just one bite
of roast pig?" he asked her.

"Greedy beggar!"
she yelled.
"We gave you water
and a place to sleep.
Now you ask for more!
Give me another onion!"

Felix put a second onion
on her plate.
She ate it, too, and
asked for another.
Felix gave her
the third onion.

He ate the last one.
Then he curled up
next to the dogs
and went to sleep.

In the night
Felix heard a noise.
"Oh, I am dying!"
the woman cried.
"That beggar
has poisoned me
with his onions."

The farmer chased
Felix from the house.
"I will ride to the city
to tell the judge
what you have done.
He will see that you hang,"
he shouted.

Chapter Three

The Mule's Tail

Felix went to the city
to find the judge.
He had seen
the farmer and Marcos
ride past him
on their horses
early that day.

Felix saw a man.
His mule was stuck
in the mud.
Felix stepped
behind the mule.
"I will twist his tail.
You pull while I push,"
he told the man.

"One, two, THREE!"

Felix counted.

HEEEEE ARRRRRRR!

The mule jumped

onto the dry road.

But his tail was

still in Felix's hand.

"Look what you did!"
the man yelled.
"Now the mule is no good!
I will ride to the city
to tell the judge."

The man rode off.

"You will hang!"

he yelled at Felix.

"They can only hang me once,"
Felix told himself.
"But once is
  surely enough."

Chapter Four

In The City

It was dark
when Felix got
to the city.
He had no money
to pay for a room.
So he crawled
to the top of a wall
and went to sleep.

But Felix forgot
he was on a wall.
He tossed in his sleep
and fell off.
"Ie—eeeeeeeye!"
he yelled.
He fell on a napping horse.

The horse kicked

a sleeping dog.

The dog snapped
at a dozing cat.

The cat scratched the nose
of a sleeping man.

The man yelled.
He jumped up,
kicking the wall
with his bare toe.

The man rubbed
his sore toe
and his sore nose.
"You almost killed me!"
he yelled at Felix.
"I will tell the judge!"

Felix shrugged.

"They can only hang me once.

But once is enough,"

he said.

Chapter Five

The Judge

In court the next day,
Marcos spoke first.
Then Felix showed
the piece of paper
to the judge.
The judge said,
"The house belongs
to Felix."

He made Marcos give
1000 gold coins to Felix
for his trouble.

VOTE
ROUNDS
FOR
SHERIFF

Felix bowed.
There were still three men
to speak to the judge.
But now his family had
a house and money for food.

When the farmer finished
his story, the judge asked him,
"Did your wife die?"
The farmer said,
"I was in a hurry
to get here.
I did not look to see."

The judge hid a smile.
"Your greedy wife
is not dead.
But she will not eat
too many onions again."

He made the farmer give
500 gold coins to Felix
for his trouble.

But two men still waited
to speak to the judge.
The man with the mule
told his tale next.

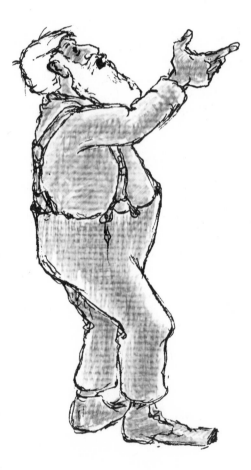

The judge almost laughed.
"Felix did hurt the mule.
He should be punished
for that," he said.
"He must keep the mule
until its tail grows back."

"But, judge!" the man said.
"A mule's tail will not
grow back."

The judge smiled.

"Oh? Is that so?

Then it serves Felix right.

He will have to look after

the mule for the rest

of its life."

He made the man give
250 gold coins to Felix
for his trouble.

Felix bowed low.

Now his family had a house,

1750 gold coins and

a mule to ride.

But the angry man
with the sore nose
and the sore toe
still waited.

The judge said
his story was
the worst of all.
"This man must
have justice," he said.

"He must stand on the wall.

Then he will jump on the horse.

The horse will kick the dog.

The dog will bite the cat.

The cat will then
scratch Felix.

And Felix will run
into the wall."

The man hopped
on his good foot.
His nose grew redder.

"But the fall will kill me!
I am not like Felix.
Felix is a lucky man!"

The judge laughed.
"If you will not jump,
you must pay Felix
50 gold coins."

Felix rode home
on his mule.
His pockets jingled
with coins.

And the words of the man
rang in his ears.
He was truly a lucky man.

MARY BLOUNT CHRISTIAN has written over thirty books for young readers, including "The Goosehill Gang Mysteries," and *Devin and Goliath* and *The First Sign of Winter.* She was the creator and moderator of the syndicated PBS-TV series, "Children's Bookshelf." Mary Christian currently teaches writing at the Community College in Houston, Texas, her home town.

GLEN ROUNDS is one of the most popular illustrators of children's picture books in the United States, and the author-artist of numerous books of his own. Among these are: *Knute, the Giant Bullsnake; The Day the Circus Came to Lone Tree; Ol' Paul, the Mighty Logger* and *The Blind Colt.* Glen Rounds grew up in the West but now lives in North Carolina.

Ready for fun?
Laugh with Ready-to-Read rib-ticklers.

5 MEN UNDER 1 UMBRELLA
And Other Ready-to-Read Riddles
Written and illustrated by Joseph Low
Thirty ridiculous riddles will keep beginning readers on their toes. "An enjoyable addition to the abundant volumes of riddle lore." *—Horn Book*

HOMER THE HUNTER
By Richard J. Margolis/Illustrated by Leonard Kessler
The animals Homer the hunter thinks he has killed come back to "haunt" him. "Kids will love 'Oooooooooooing' with the ghosts and find the text easy and satisfying." *—School Library Journal*

GRANNY AND THE INDIANS
By Peggy Parish/Illustrated by Brinton Turkle
Spunky Granny Guntry drives her neighbors, the Indians, frantic in "an original, truly funny story...." *—Horn Book*

GRANNY AND THE DESPERADOES
By Peggy Parish/Illustrated by Steven Kellogg
Granny Guntry confronts two pie-stealing desperadoes with rib-tickling results!

GRANNY, THE BABY, AND THE BIG GRAY THING
By Peggy Parish/Illustrated by Lynn Sweat
The Indians think near-sighted Granny is going to feed their baby to a wolf. "The confusion that results makes a droll and sprightly story." *—Publishers Weekly*

TOO MANY RABBITS
By Peggy Parish/Illustrated by Leonard Kessler
How many rabbits are too many? Kind-hearted Miss Molly finds out soon enough when she takes in one stray. "Will delight primary readers."
—School Library Journal

THE GOLLYWHOPPER EGG
Written and illustrated by Anne Rockwell
Country peddler Timothy Todd sells a coconut as a gollywhopper egg and Farmer Foote tries to hatch it. "Fun and good humor...."
—School Library Journal (starred review)

A BEAR, A BOBCAT AND THREE GHOSTS
Written and illustrated by Anne Rockwell
Timothy Todd joins a moonlit Halloween chase, and "beginning readers get a comic and mysterious *Ready-to-Read*." *—Publishers Weekly*

TIMOTHY TODD'S GOOD THINGS ARE GONE
Written and illustrated by Anne Rockwell
The peddler's pack disappears, and he sets out to find the thief. Surprises in store will delight beginning readers.